P9-BZX-860

Fairy Felicity's Moonlight Adventure

Alison Murray

One warm summer night, at the end of the day,
the fairies awoke and were ready to play.
When Fairy Felicity opened her door,
she spotted a letter, right there on the floor.
The message said, “Follow the silvery snail.
You’ll find a surprise at the end of the trail!”

“I’m here!” called the snail.
“Come on! Quick, let’s go!”
“Gosh,” said the fairy.
“I thought snails were slow!”

She followed the
snail trail wherever it led.
"But where will it take me?"
Felicity said.

A moth joined in too, and they flew through the night,
tracking the snail trail, all sparkly and bright.

and met a bright ladybug covered in dots.

Then down in the orchard
they flew through the trees
and on past the hives
all a-buzzing with bees.

“Oh, Dragonfly, join us!” Felicity said . . .

as Moth, Bee, and Ladybug raced on ahead.

They wove through the foxgloves
and circled the roses
and hopped over daisies that
tickled their noses.

At the end of the garden
they came to a wall
where the ivy was thick and
the grass was quite tall.

And there, by an old door,
the snail stopped and said,
"This way, Miss Felicity—
please watch your head."

She crept through the gap
where the dandelions grew . . .

"Surprise!"
cried her friends.

"Happy Birthday
to you!"

For Carole

First U.S. edition 2016

Library of Congress Catalog Card Number 2015941705
ISBN 978-0-7636-8945-2

16 17 18 19 20 21 SFP 10 9 8 7 6 5 4 3 2 1

Printed in Shenzhen, Guangdong, China

This book was typeset in Cremona.
The illustrations were created digitally.

Nosy Crow
an imprint of
Candlewick Press
99 Dover Street
Somerville, Massachusetts 02144

www.nosycrow.com
www.candlewick.com